MW01004372

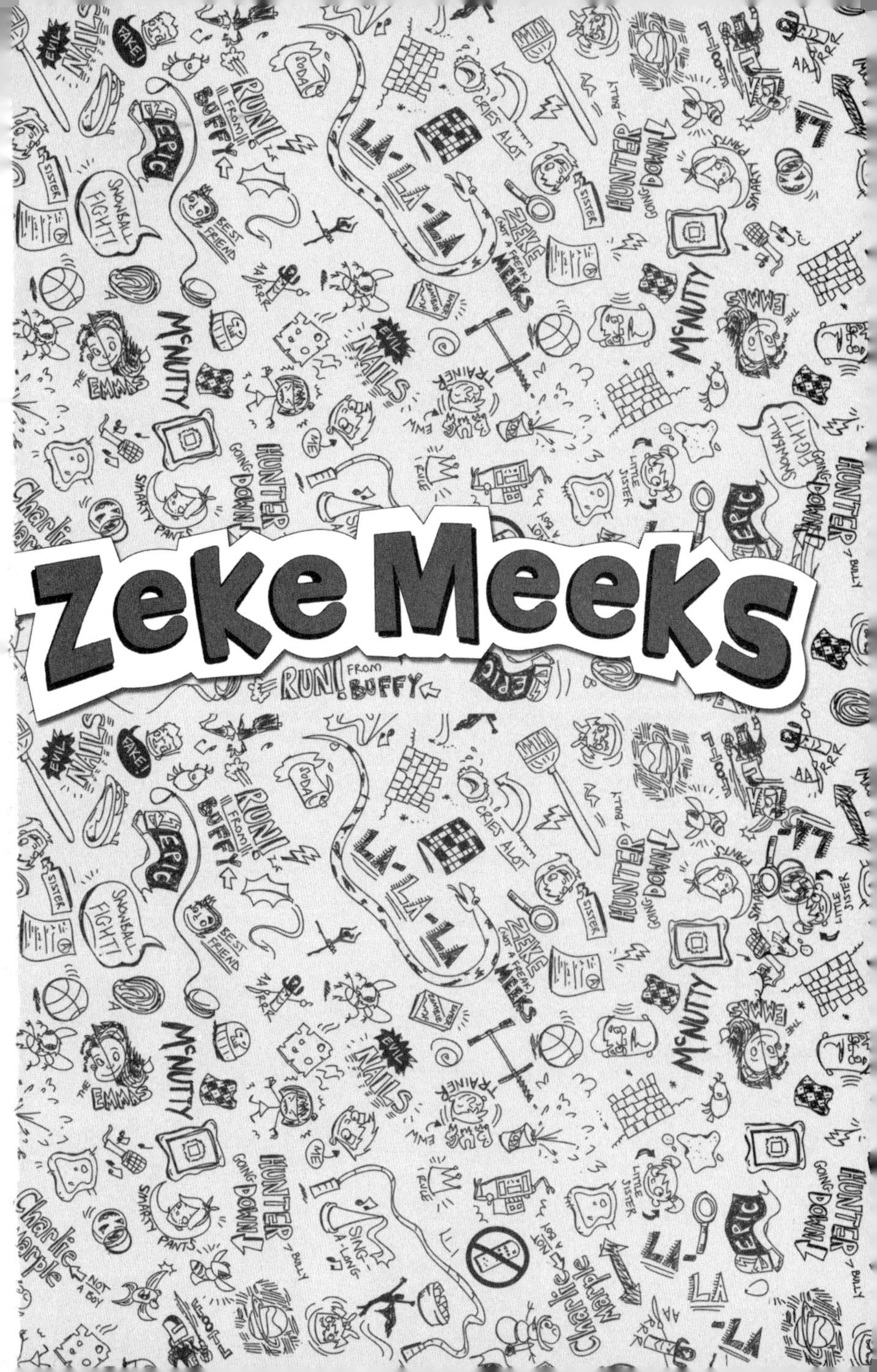
Zeke Meeks

HATS LIKE THIS REALLY
AREN'T MY THING.

Zeke Meeks is published by
Picture Window Books
A Capstone Imprint
1710 Roe Crest Drive
North Mankato, MN 56003
www.capstoneyoungreaders.com

Library of Congress Cataloging in Publication Data
Green, D. L. (Debra L.)
   Zeke Meeks vs the big blah-rific birthday / by D. L. Green; illustrated by Josh Alves.
      p. cm. — (Zeke Meeks)
   Summary: Zeke Meeks will be nine soon, but he is not looking forward to a party that
his sisters want to take over and nobody but his closest friends want to attend — but the
alternative is going to Grace Chang's party on the same day, and she is really scary.
   ISBN 978-1-4048-8105-1 (hard cover)
   1. Birthday parties—Juvenile fiction. 2. Middle-born children—Juvenile fiction. 3. Brothers
and sisters—Juvenile fiction. 4. Friendship—Juvenile fiction. [1. Birthdays—Fiction. 2. Parties—
Fiction. 3. Middle-born children—Fiction. 4. Brothers and sisters—Fiction. 5. Friendship—
Fiction. 6. Humorous stories.] I. Alves, Josh, ill. II. Title. III. Title: Zeke Meeks versus the
big blah-rific birthday. IV. Series: Green, D. L. (Debra L.) Zeke Meeks.
   PZ7.G81926Zdm 2013
   813.6—dc23   2012028191

Vector Credits: Shutterstock
Book design by K. Fraser

Printed in the United States of America
in Stevens Point, Wisconsin.
092012   006937WZS13

MY DOG WAGGLES.
HIS FAVORITE PART OF
A PARTY IS THE CAKE!

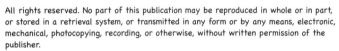

Zeke Meeks

vs THE BIG BLAH-RIFIC BIRTHDAY

BY D. L. GREEN

ILLUSTRATED BY JOSH ALVES

PICTURE WINDOW BOOKS
a capstone imprint

← My dog Waggles wearing a bonnet. This will be explained. I promise.

TABLE OF

CHAPTER 1:

Dancing, <u>Kissing</u>, and Other Horrible Things 6

↳ Gross! Why would anybody want to do that?

CHAPTER 2:

Isn't Recess Supposed to Be <u>Fun</u>? 18

↳ It used to be my favorite subject!

CHAPTER 3:

A <u>BIG</u> Problem 30

CHAPTER 4:

My Boring Birthday Bummer... 40

CHAPTER 5:

Hurray for <u>Blood</u> and Gore! 50

← That might be what you think it is.

BOYS RULE EVERYTHING BUT THE PLAYGROUND

← My party invites. Kind of a failure.

CONTENTS

CHAPTER 6:

At Least Rudy Morse Liked It 60

CHAPTER 7:

Who Doesn't Like a SURPRISE PARTY? My Mom, That's

Who! 78

CHAPTER 8:

Guess Who Else Doesn't Like a SURPRISE Party? 86

CHAPTER 9:

The Presence and Presents of Grace 98

CHAPTER 10:

Laundry Folding: Almost as Good as Thrillsville 110

I do fear for my life.

↳ and sharp fingernails

↳ Laundry folding can be fun! No, really!
   Read on, and you'll see.

My popular friend Owen
sure knows how to create
scheduling problems.

GIRLS DROOL ALL BUT GRACE — SHE BITES

Dancing, Kissing, and Other Horrible Things

"Oh good, Zeke. You're dead," my little sister, Mia, said.

I sat slumped on the couch. I had just been killed by a hairy mutant in my *Morbid Monster* video game. I had fought off tiger-bats, shrieking mummies, and six sets of giant, chomping fangs. It was great.

Mia grabbed the remote control. "Now that you're dead, it's my turn for the TV. I want to watch the *Princess Sing-Along* show."

My older sister, Alexa, looked up from her *Totally Cute Boys* magazine. She said, "After *Princess Sing-Along*, I want to watch *The Real Lives of Extremely Rich and Nasty Teen Girls*. It's my favorite show. Mimsy and her friend Maisy already have matching motorboats and sports cars. On this week's show, they'll shop for airplanes."

I didn't want to watch the *Princess Sing-Along* show or *The Real Lives of Extremely Rich and Nasty Teen Girls*, so I walked into the kitchen.

Mom was washing dishes. She said, "Zeke, you'll be nine years old soon. We need to plan your birthday party."

"When I turn nine, I'll be more mature. I should get a later bedtime and a bigger allowance," I said.

"You're right. You will be more mature," Mom said.

I smiled. I'd use my extra allowance money to buy video games. With my new bedtime, I'd stay up late playing video games.

"That doesn't mean you'll get a later bedtime or a bigger allowance. But when you're a mature nine-year-old, you'll be able to do more chores," Mom said as she scrubbed a frying pan.

I frowned and went back into the living room.

Mia turned the channel on the TV. The *Princess Sing-Along* show was starting. Princess Sing-Along said, "Hello, dear friends. Let's get started on a super-duper song."

Ugh. I put my hands over my ears. But I still heard Princess Sing-Along's awful song: "Eat lots of healthy food that's green, la la la. Veggies, not your boogers, I mean, la la la."

"Zeke, you should have a Princess Sing-Along birthday party," Mia said.

"No, thanks." I would rather spend my birthday alone.

"You could play Pin the Skirt on the Princess and eat pretty, pink cupcakes and give your guests sparkly necklaces."

"No, thanks." I would rather spend my birthday alone in a hole in the ground.

"You could have a birthday party with dancing," Alexa said.

"No, thanks." I would rather spend my birthday alone in a hole in the ground in a snowstorm.

"You could take a few friends to the art museum," Mom said as she dusted the living room furniture.

"No, thanks." I would rather spend my birthday alone in a hole in the ground in a snowstorm in the dark.

Girls might like Princess Sing-Along, dancing, and art museums. But I didn't.

I was so tired of girls and their girly things. They were all around me. Alexa was cutting out a picture of the Totally Cutest Boy of the Month from her magazine. My mom was dusting a china doll. Mia sang along with Princess Sing-Along: "Even a lovely queen, la la la, must keep her body clean, la la la. So wash away your dirt and grime, la la la, before it turns to stinky slime, la la la."

I wished my dad were here. He was a soldier, away on a top secret mission.

The only other guy in my family was our dog, Waggles. I called him over.

Waggles ran into the room. Oh, no.

He was wearing a purple bonnet on his head.

"Don't you love the pretty new hat I got for Waggles?" Mia said.

I shook my head. "Waggles is a boy dog. Boys don't like pretty stuff. And they don't like parties with Princess Sing-Along or dancing or art museums."

On TV, a commercial came on for Thrillsville Amusement Park. Thrillsville had amazing shows, wild roller coasters, and lots of junk food and gift shops.

I pointed to the TV. "I want to go there for my birthday."

"Thrillsville costs a lot of money. But I suppose you could take a few friends there on your birthday," Mom said.

"Thanks," I said.

I figured my guest list in my head. "I'll
invite the twelve boys in my class, a few girls
I'm friends with, and some neighbors. So I'll
take about twenty kids to Thrillsville."

"Twenty! If you want to invite all those
people, have a party at home," Mom said.

I crossed my arms. "That's so unfair. A party
at home would be boring."

"We can make it fun," Mom said.

I thought about that for a minute. "Okay. We'll hire a magician and a juggler and someone to make balloon animals. And we can rent a bounce house for the backyard. It'll be almost as good as Thrillsville."

"Do you have any idea how much that would cost?" Mom asked.

"Of course not. I'm a kid," I said.

"It would cost a fortune. We'll have a nice, simple party for you instead. You and your friends can run around in the backyard, play a few games, and eat cake."

"Pink cupcakes are nice and simple," Mia said.

"Dancing is nice and simple," Alexa said. "Well, dancing with Bruno Burnside isn't nice and simple. He tries to kiss people he dances with. And no one wants to kiss Bruno Burnside."

"You kissed a boy?" Mom asked her.

Alexa's cheeks turned red. She mumbled, "Oh, I just heard that from a friend."

"Yuck," I said.

"Zeke, you'll love dancing with girls when you get older," Alexa said.

"I will never love dancing with girls, even when I'm 102 years old. I don't want a dancing party," I said. "And a nice, simple party at home sounds awful. If turning nine means having a boring party and doing more chores, I don't even want to get older!"

I ran into my room and slammed the door.

Isn't Recess Supposed to Be Fun?

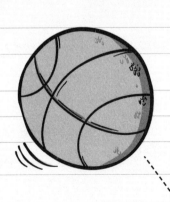

I felt happier at school the next day. I wasn't happy about sitting quietly at my desk. I wasn't happy about listening to my teacher. I wasn't happy about learning things. But I was happy to see my friends.

At recess, I played basketball with my best friend, Hector Cruz. I made five baskets in a row. I felt very happy about that. Neither Hector nor I had ever made six baskets in a row. If I could land another one, I'd break our record. Maybe I'd even set a school record.

I carefully held the ball in the middle of my palms. I raised my hands over my head. I crooked my elbows. I bent my knees. I was in perfect position. This was it. I was ready to shoot the ball. Hopefully, I was about to shatter my all-time basketball shooting record.

Just as I started to shoot the ball, something horrible and scary happened. It wasn't just horrible and scary. It was horribly scary. It was also scarily horrible.

Are you ready to read this? I hope you're sitting down and clutching your favorite stuffed animal or video game.

Are you sure you're ready to read about this horribly scary and scarily horrible thing?

Okay, here goes:

A big fly flew near me.

I hope you didn't just faint or cry or call for your mommy. I really hope you didn't just do two or more of these things.

I didn't faint or cry or call for my mommy. But I wanted to do all three.

I missed my basketball shot. Then I ran away from the horribly scary and scarily horrible fly. I raced through the playground as fast as I could.

I'm terrified of flies. I'm also terrified of bees, grasshoppers, spiders, moths, butterflies, gnats, ladybugs, beetles, crickets, ants, wasps, fleas, and every other bug in the universe. It's embarrassing. Please don't tell anyone.

Hector ran after me, calling out, "What's wrong, Zeke?"

I didn't want him to know that I was scared of a fly. I also didn't want to lie. So I told Hector something true: "I'm upset that my birthday party will be just a simple party at home."

"That's too bad," Hector said. "But look on the bright side. When you turn nine, you'll get a bigger allowance and a later bedtime."

"No, I won't. My mom said that when I turn nine, I'll just get more chores."

"Too bad for you, Zeke the Freak Meeks," Grace Chang sneered.

The only thing more terrifying than insects was Grace Chang. She was short and skinny and evil. She had long, thick fingernails as sharp as knives. They were evil too.

"Yeah, too bad for you, Zeke the Freak Meeks," Emma G. said.

"Yeah, too bad for you, Zeke the Freak Meeks," Emma J. said.

Emma G. and Emma J. were also short and skinny. But they weren't terrifying or evil. They were just copycats.

Grace was known to rip people's faces off. So I took a step back and covered my face with my hands.

"Relax. Your birthday is coming up. I wouldn't rip off the face of the birthday boy," she said.

Oh, great. I let out a relieved sigh.

"I'll wait until after your birthday," she said.

Oh, great. I let out a sad sigh. As soon as I turned nine, Mom would give me more chores and Grace would give me a face-ripping. I wished I could stay eight forever.

"My birthday is coming up also. My parents said they'll raise my allowance to twenty dollars a week. And they'll let me stay up until ten o'clock every night," Grace said. "I'm so lucky."

"Yeah, you're so lucky," Emma G. said.

"Yeah, you're so lucky," Emma J. said.

"I'm going to have a birthday party at my house," Grace said.

"Sorry to hear that. I'm having a party at home too," I said.

"Will there be a bunch of entertainers, a fun money toss game, and an entire table filled with food?" Grace asked.

"Yeah, will there?" Emma G. asked.

"Yeah, will there?" Emma J. asked.

"There will be cake," I said.

"I'm serving cake and apple pie and lots of other desserts. Will your party have all that?" Grace asked.

"Yeah, will it?" Emma G. asked.

"Yeah, will it?" Emma J. asked.

I shook my head and walked away.

Owen Leach tapped me on the shoulder. He said, "I heard your birthday is coming up. Mine is too. I can't wait to turn nine. I'm getting a raise in my allowance to twenty-five dollars a week. And I'll get to stay up until ten thirty every night. My party will be at Thrillsville."

"You must be inviting only a few kids," I said.

"Nope. I'm inviting everyone in the class. It's the Sunday after next."

I started to tell him that my party was going to be on that day. But he couldn't hear me. Everyone around us was chanting, "Yay for Thrillsville! Yay for Owen! Yay for Thrillsville! Yay for Owen! Yay for Thrillsville! Yay for Owen! Yay for Thrillsville! Yay for Owen!" And so on.

I'd have to change the date of my party. No one would go to my house instead of Thrillsville.

I sighed. I sure was having a bad day. I'd missed my chance to set a basketball shooting record. I'd found out that Grace and Owen were getting bigger allowances, later bedtimes, and better parties than me. Also, Grace said she planned to rip my face off after my birthday.

There was only one good thing about today: I had escaped from the horribly scary, scarily horrible fly.

Then the fly landed on me.

A BIG Problem

I sat at the kitchen table after school. While I ate cookies and drank milk, Mom started cleaning the oven. I told her, "Owen Leach is having a party at Thrillsville on the day of my party. He's inviting the whole class. You have to change the date on the invitations."

"You're old enough to change the invitations yourself," she said.

"Me?" I asked.

"Yes, you. Change the date to a week from Saturday."

So I had to take all the invitations out of their envelopes. Then I had to change the date from Sunday to Saturday. Then I had to put all the invitations back in their envelopes. That took six whole, entire minutes. "I'm so worn out after all that work," I told Mom.

She didn't hear me. Her head was in the oven as she scrubbed it clean.

I heard the mail truck stop near our house. I asked Mom, "Can you give Mrs. Perez my invitations to mail out?" Mrs. Perez was our postal worker.

"You're old enough to give her the invitations yourself," Mom said.

I wasn't even nine yet, and I was already tired of being old enough to do things myself. But I ran outside anyway.

My sister Mia followed me.

Our dog, Waggles, followed us.

I gave Mrs. Perez my invitations to mail.

She smiled and said, "You are getting to be such a big boy."

Then she patted Mia's head and said, "What a darling little girl." She gave Mia a lollipop.

Next, she patted Waggles's head and said, "What a sweet pup." She gave him a dog biscuit.

"I love sweet things to eat," I said. I hoped Mrs. Perez would take the hint.

She smiled again. "I have something for you."

I smiled back at her. I wondered what kind of candy Mrs. Perez would give me. I hoped I'd get a chocolate bar.

"It's heavy. Are you strong enough to carry it?" she asked me.

I licked my lips as I pictured a gigantic and very yummy chocolate bar. "I can handle it, Mrs. Perez," I said in my most mature voice.

"Here it is." She handed me a large pile of mail.

I frowned and walked back to the house with my hands full of envelopes.

Mia followed me. Her hands were full of lollipop.

Waggles followed us. His mouth was full of dog biscuit and slobber.

M _

I gave Mom the mail. She sighed and said, "Bills, bills, bills, bills, bills."

Then she handed me a big envelope. It was addressed to "Zeke the Freak Meeks."

I opened it and pulled out a large, pink piece of paper. A bunch of purple glitter fell out of the envelope. It got all over me and Waggles and the floor.

"What a mess," I said.

Mom pointed to a broom. "No problem. Clean up the glitter."

"It's a problem. I don't like cleaning."

"Clean it anyway," Mom said.

First I read the pink paper. It said:

BEST BIRTHDAY PARTY EVER!

9

GRACE CHANG TURNS NINE!

MAGICIANS! FACE PAINTERS! MUSIC!
MONEY TOSS GAME!
GREAT FOOD AND DESSERTS!
YOU AND EVERYONE ELSE IN
MY CLASS ARE INVITED

MY PARTY WILL LAST
ALL DAY AND NIGHT.

MAKE SURE YOU BRING A GOOD GIFT.
"GOOD" MEANS SOMETHING THAT COSTS A LOT OF MONEY.

Even though it was a party for evil Grace Chang, it sounded like a lot of fun. I couldn't wait to go.

I wondered how long I would have to wait to go. I looked at the invitation again and saw the date of the party. Oh, no. "Grace's party is on the same day as mine," I said.

"No problem," Mom said. "We'll have your party at a different time."

"It's a problem. Grace's party is all day and night."

I ran outside to take back my invitations from Mrs. Perez.

I looked up and down the block. But I didn't see the mail truck anywhere.

Sadly, I returned to my house.

Mom handed me a broom and told me to sweep up all the glitter.

Mia took her lollipop out of her mouth and said, "Poor Zeke. Here's a nice song to cheer you up."

Before I could say, "No," or, "Please don't," or, "I beg you to stop," Mia broke into a Princess Sing-Along song: "You look silly when you pout, la la la. You sound yucky when you shout, la la la. Be sweet as a violin, la la la. And put on a lovely grin, la la la."

I didn't care how yucky I sounded. I shouted, "I can't stand Princess Sing-Along songs! And I can't stand birthdays!"

My Boring Birthday Bummer

IT'S NOT WHAT YOU THINK.
I SWEAR. KEEP READING
THIS CHAPTER.

The next morning at school, everyone gathered around Owen Leach and Grace Chang. Owen said, "Next weekend will be fantastic. Grace's party is on Saturday and my party is on Sunday."

"It was very nice of you and Grace to invite the entire class to your parties," Laurie Schneider said.

"I invited everyone so I could keep being the most popular boy in third grade," Owen said.

"I invited everyone so I could get as many presents as possible," Grace said.

I cleared my throat. Then I said, "Grace, is your party really going to last all day and night? That's a long time. People might want to go to other parties on Saturday."

"It will take all day and night to do all the fun things and eat all the great food at my party. No one will want to go anywhere else," Grace said.

"People will want to be at my party at Thrillsville all day and night too," Owen said.

I sighed. They were right. And no one would want to spend one minute at my party.

Rudy Morse said, "I can't wait to go on the Spin-Hurtle-Drop ride at Thrillsville. It makes people puke their guts out."

Victoria Crow looked up from the encyclopedia she was reading. "Super smart people like me don't care about emesis."

"What's emesis?" Rudy asked.

"Vomit," Victoria said.

Rudy scratched his head. "I thought I knew all the words for vomit: puke, barf, ralph, yack, gack, hurl, launch lunch, blow chunks, yodel groceries, and — my personal favorite — laugh at the toilet. Thanks for giving me a new word: emesis. That's cool."

"I don't think it's cool. All this talk about vomit is making me sick," Laurie Schneider said. She ran to the nearest trash can.

Unfortunately, she didn't reach the nearest trash can on time.

Even more unfortunately, she reached Mr. McNutty, our teacher.

Can you guess what happened next?

This is what happened: Laurie Schneider threw up all over Mr. McNutty. In other words, she puked, barfed, ralphed, yacked, gacked, hurled, launched lunch, blew chunks, yodeled groceries, emitted emesis, and — Rudy Morse's personal favorite — laughed at the toilet.

"Yuck. Gross. Eww," Mr. McNutty said.

"Cool!" Rudy said.

Laurie wiped her mouth with a tissue.

"I feel better now," she said.

"I feel worse now," Mr. McNutty said.

I bet you can't guess what happened next.

This is what happened: Mr. McNutty bent down to clean the vomit from his pants and shoes. Bending down made his hairpiece fall off.

Can you guess where his hairpiece landed?

This is where Mr. McNutty's hairpiece landed: in the mound of Laurie's vomit.

"Super cool!" Rudy said. "I hope everyone stuffs their faces with food and desserts at Grace's party and then throws up there too."

Laurie patted her stomach. "This new talk about throwing up is making me feel sick again."

Mr. McNutty shouted, "Uh-oh!" Then he grabbed his puke-soaked hairpiece and ran away.

My best friend, Hector, turned to me and said, "Your birthday is coming up too."

I nodded. "I didn't know Grace's party was on the same day as mine. I'm having a house party too. But there won't be much food or entertainment."

"Sorry, Grace. I'm going to Zeke's party. I'm his best friend," Hector said.

"Sorry, Grace. I'm going to Zeke's party too. I'm his second best friend," said Charlie Marple. It was true: even though she's a girl she was my second best friend.

Everyone else said they were going to Grace's party.

I didn't blame them. Grace's party sounded like a lot more fun than mine.

"Kids want to go to my booming birthday bash, not your boring birthday bummer," Grace said. "But don't worry. I'll give you something special after your birthday."

"A gift?" I asked.

She waved her long, sharp, evil fingernails in front of me. Then she laughed evilly. "You'll be getting a special gift of nails in your face."

I shuddered.

Hurray for Blood and Gore!

No matter how bad birthdays get there is always CAKE!

YUM!

HAPPY B-DAY ZEKE

After school, I lay on the hammock in the backyard. Mia sat on a swing with her Princess Sing-Along doll. Mom stood on the grass, raking leaves. "I have it so hard," I said as I swung gently in the hammock.

Mom put down the rake and wiped her sweaty forehead. "What's wrong?" she asked.

"The only people coming to my birthday party are Hector and Charlie."

"It's better to have a few close friends than to know a lot of people who aren't close friends," Mom said. "Besides, I'll be at your party too, because I'm your mom. And Alexa will be there because . . ." She didn't finish the sentence.

"Because Mom is making Alexa go to your party," Mia said.

I sighed.

"Don't worry. I'll be at your party too," Mia said. "And so will Princess Sing-Along. We can entertain everyone with our favorite songs."

I did not want to hear Princess Sing-Along songs at my birthday party or anywhere else. I told Mia, "Princess Sing-Along and I had a chat yesterday."

Mia's mouth dropped open in surprise. "Really?"

I nodded. "Really. Princess Sing-Along told me she's very shy. She wants to stay in your bedroom during the party. She also said you shouldn't sing her songs so much. And when you do, you should sing them very softly."

"Like this?" Mia asked. She started singing very softly. But her voice got louder and louder. By the end of the song, she was screeching the words.

I covered my ears, but heard the song anyway.

"If you decide to drink, la la la, soda in a big glass, la la la, just know that you may stink, la la la. Soda can give you gas, la la la."

"Stop!" I shouted. "Princess Sing-Along doesn't like when you sing so loud."

Mia shook her head. "Princess Sing-Along told me she loves when I sing loud. We're going to sing extra loud at your party."

"My party is going to be awful. Grace's party will be a lot better. I've just decided to cancel my party. Hector, Charlie, and I can go to Grace's house instead," I said.

Someone knocked on the gate to our backyard. Mom walked to the gate and opened it for Hector.

He headed over to me, holding a wrapped present. He said, "You had a hard day. Here's an early birthday gift to cheer you up."

I unwrapped my present. It was a *Bloody Gore* video game. I said, "Wow, thanks! Blood and gore are perfect ways to cheer me up."

Hector smiled. "Blood and gore always make me happy too."

Then Charlie walked over from her house across the street. She handed me a box and said, "I hope this will cheer you up."

I opened the box. It was a chocolate cake with chocolate frosting. "Happy B-Day Zeke" was spelled out in mini marshmallows.

Charlie said, "I asked my dad to bake you a chocolate cake with marshmallows on it. I know that's your favorite kind of cake."

"That is so cool. Thanks," I said.

Mia sang another Princess Sing-Along song: "Chocolate cake is very nice, la la la. But don't have more than a slice, la la la. Eating too much chocolate, la la la, could make all your teeth rot, la la la."

Hector, Charlie, and I rolled our eyes.

"And now I'll sing ten more Princess Sing-Along songs," Mia said. She started to sing, "When you poop —"

Hector, Charlie, and I threw Mia and her Princess Sing-Along doll into a big pile of leaves.

We all laughed.

Luckily, Mom and Mia laughed too.

And most importantly, Mia stopped singing.

Hector and Charlie's plans to cheer me up had worked. I felt a lot better. I hated to admit it, but Mom might have been right. Maybe it really was better to have a few close friends than to have a bunch of friends you didn't know very well.

Plus, there were only a few people to share my birthday cake with. We each got to eat a huge slice. That chocolate marshmallow cake was yummy.

At Least Rudy Morse Liked It

THE QUEEN
OF LONG,
SHARP, EVIL
FINGERNAILS!

Mom took me to the mall to get a birthday present for Grace. We bought her a jigsaw puzzle.

"You should give her something else too. Does she like dolls?" Mom asked.

I shrugged. "Grace probably likes ripping faces off dolls with her long, sharp, evil fingernails."

"We could get her a Frisbee," Mom said.

I shook my head. "Grace won't play with Frisbees. She's worried about breaking her long, sharp, evil fingernails."

"We could get her a book. What would Grace like to read about?" Mom asked.

"Face ripping," I said.

Mom sighed.

We spent a long time searching the mall for a good gift. Finally, I found something perfect for Grace: nail polish. We bought her a bottle of bright pink polish to show off her long, sharp, evil fingernails.

Even though I had canceled my own birthday party, I was excited to go to Grace's party. I woke up very early and skipped breakfast that day. I wanted extra room in my stomach for all the great food and desserts at Grace's house.

I got ready quickly. I even brushed my teeth and hair without Mom telling me to.

"It's cold out. Wear a hat and gloves," Mom said as we were leaving.

"I don't need to. I'm sure Grace's house will be warm," I said. It would take me a minute to get my hat and gloves. I didn't want to miss one minute of Grace's party.

Mom dropped me off at the front curb. I walked up a long driveway to Grace's very large house. It was a chilly day. I couldn't wait to get inside.

A sign at the front door said, "Party is in the backyard."

I went to the gate on the side of Grace's house and opened it.

Grace stood in front of me. She had a big, pink butterfly on her face.

A bug! Yikes! I felt like fainting, crying, or calling for my mommy. But if I did, I'd probably get teased every day for the next fifty years.

Instead, I pointed my trembling finger at the horrible butterfly, and said in a trembling voice, "There's a gigantic insect on your face."

Grace scowled. "You're dumb. That's not a real butterfly. It's a picture of a butterfly. I just got my face painted."

Phew. A picture of a butterfly wasn't completely terrifying. But it was still a little terrifying.

Grace pointed to the present in my hands and said, "Hand it over."

I handed it over.

"If that present isn't good, I'll rip your face off," she said.

I looked around, hoping to find someone to help me and my face. There were a lot of kids at the party. The backyard fence was draped with huge pictures of Grace. A sign on the back door leading to the house said, "Do not enter."

"Are we staying outside the whole time?" I asked. I was shivering from the cold weather and from being near Grace.

"Of course we're staying outside," Grace said. "I don't want footprints on my rug or fingerprints on my furniture. My house is too beautiful to allow guests in it."

"Are the entertainers here yet?" I asked.

"That's the musician." Grace pointed to an old man holding a flute and sleeping under a tree.

"Where are the good entertainers?" I asked.

Grace waved her long, sharp, evil fingernails at me.

"Are you insulting my party?" she asked.

I shook my head. Then I put my hands over my face to try to protect it.

Grace pointed to a woman in a long white coat. "That's the face painter."

I walked over to her. Laurie Schneider was getting her face painted with a pink butterfly like Grace's. A line of girls waited behind her. A group of boys stood nearby.

"Don't you guys want a turn with the face painter?" I asked the boys.

"The only thing she's painting is pink butterflies. Yuck," Rudy Morse said.

"Yuck," I repeated.

Then a man in a black cape announced, "I am Morlon the Magnificent. My magic show is starting."

Finally, a good entertainer. We all sat on the lawn to watch the show.

Morlon waved a plastic wand and held up a deck of cards. He pointed to Grace and said, "Name a card."

"I like diamonds because they're almost as sharp as my nails," she said. "And I like queens because I always act like a queen. So I choose the queen of diamonds."

Morlon waved his wand again. Then he threw all the cards on the ground and said, "Ta-da! Your queen of diamonds is in there somewhere."

Everyone groaned.

Morlon held up a cup of punch and said, "I will make this disappear."

He waved his wand, drank the punch, and said, "Ta-da! The punch has disappeared."

A few people started booing.

"Wait." Morlon put his hand in the pocket of his cape. He pulled out his wallet. Then he took a penny from it. He asked for a volunteer. No one wanted to volunteer.

So Morlon walked over to Hector and waved his wand at him. He put his hand behind Hector's ear and held up the penny. "Ta-da!" he said.

More people booed.

The magician grabbed Grace and said, "I will saw this girl in half. I'll try to, anyway. I hope there's a hospital nearby in case something goes wrong again."

Everyone except Grace cheered.

Grace said, "Morlon, you're a moron. Make yourself disappear."

Morlon waved his wand and said, "Ta-da!" Then he ran away.

I wished I could disappear from this bad party.

Grace pointed to a long picnic table. "Time for lunch. My parents spent hundreds of dollars on fancy food. There's caviar to start with."

"What's caviar?" I asked.

"Fish eggs. We also have escargot. That's a fancy French word for snails. And we have paté. That's liver. And there are frog legs and squid. They all cost a lot of money."

I wished Morlon had made the food disappear.

The only person who ate lunch was Rudy Morse. "I love gross things," he said. He talked with his mouth full. Inside his mouth was a mixture of snails, liver, squid, and Rudy's spit. It was not a pretty sight.

"I feel like throwing up again," Laurie said. Then she threw up again. That was not a pretty sight either. At least her vomit didn't land on our teacher this time. It went all over the food table.

"This is the grossest party ever. I love it!"
Rudy exclaimed.

He was the only person who loved it. He was
the only person who even liked it.

"Time to play the money toss game," Grace
said.

Finally, something fun.

"Let's begin. Everyone toss your money at me," Grace said.

"Yeah, toss your money at Grace," Emma G. said.

"Yeah, toss your money at Grace," Emma J. said.

"No," a bunch of kids said.

Hector wouldn't even give Grace the penny he'd gotten from the magician.

Grace stomped over to the table with the presents and said, "I'd better get some good gifts." She grabbed the present from Victoria and tore off the wrapping. It was a book.

Grace threw it on the ground and said, "Reading is for school. Yuck."

She didn't like the other presents either.

She said the skirts from Emma G. and Emma J. were ugly. She said the jigsaw puzzle I'd given her was too hard. I really thought Grace would like the pink nail polish I gave her. But she complained, "That shade of pink went out of style two months ago. You gave me the worst presents ever. I'm so mad!"

Then she ran to the picnic table holding the desserts. "Time for dessert," she said.

Finally, something good, I thought.

But it wasn't time for something good. Grace was so mad that she turned over the dessert table. Everything toppled to the ground. The birthday cake got covered in grass. The apple pie became a mud pie. The orange Jell-O ring turned into hundreds of dirty, little, brown Jell-O bits.

"This party is awful," I said. "I wish I'd had a party at my house instead."

"Maybe you still can. You don't live far from here. We can walk over now," Hector said.

"I want to go to your house, Zeke," Owen Leach said.

"Me too," everyone but Grace and the Emmas said.

"It will be a surprise party," I said.

"How can it be a surprise party?" Hector asked. "You already know about it."

I frowned. "When a bunch of kids suddenly show up at my house, my mom will be completely surprised. But not in a good way."

Who Doesn't Like a SURPRISE PARTY? My Mom, That's Who!

I led Grace's party guests to my house and knocked on the door.

My sister Mia said, "Who is it?"

"It's Zeke and some other kids. Let us in."

"Mom said I shouldn't open the door to strangers. Princess Sing-Along says the same thing, except she sings it."

"I'm not a stranger. I'm your brother," I said.

"But some of the kids with you are strangers," Mia said. Then she started singing. "Don't let strangers in your house, la la la. They might punch you in your mouth, la la la. Before you could even shout, la la la, all your teeth could get knocked out, la la la."

I said, "Go get Mom."

Mom opened the door. She wore an old sweatshirt and stained sweatpants. Her hands were soapy and wet. "I was just cleaning the bathtub," she said.

We all shouted, "Surprise!"

Mom put her hand on her hip. "Ezekiel Heathcliff Meeks. What in the world is going on?" she asked.

Uh-oh. When she called me by my full name, I knew she was upset with me.

"Ezekiel Heathcliff Meeks. What a name!"
Owen Leach laughed.

A lot of other kids laughed.

I turned to them and said, "I don't want
you at my party if you're going to laugh at my
name."

"Party? Did you say party? You canceled your birthday party." Mom put her other hand on her other hip.

"Grace's party was awful, so I invited everyone here," I said.

Mom shook her head. "We don't have any food prepared or games planned."

"You said simple parties could be fun."

Mom looked at the crowd around me. "With all these kids, it wouldn't be a simple party. And I have a lot of chores to do today."

"But it's my birthday. You should be nice to me. You won't even raise my allowance or give me a later bedtime. Once Owen turns nine, he'll get twenty-five dollars a week allowance and a ten thirty bedtime."

Mom stared hard at Owen and asked, "Owen, is it true about your allowance and bedtime?"

Owen looked at the ground. Then he looked at Mom. She was still staring hard at him. When she stared hard at me like that, I always had to tell the truth.

Owen looked away. "Um," he said. "Um," he said again. "Um," he said eight more times.

Then he looked at my mom again. She was still staring hard at him.

Finally, Owen said, "No, Mrs. Meeks, it's not actually true. I only get a dollar a week and I have to be in bed by eight o'clock."

"That's what I thought," Mom said. "Thank you for telling the truth. But I can't hold a party here today. I have too many chores to do. I don't have time to bake a cake or organize games."

Then she closed the front door, leaving my friends and me outside in the cold.

Guess Who Else Doesn't Like a SURPRISE Party?

I stood outside with my friends. I was pretty sure they were mad at me.

"You said we could have a party at your house. We walked all the way over here. Now we can't even get inside. I'm mad at you," Laurie said.

Other people said, "Me too," or, "I'm mad at you too," or, "Grr," or, "Oof." I was pretty sure "Grr" and "Oof" both meant "I'm mad at you too."

What a horrible day. The weather had gotten even colder. I had been wrong not to wear a hat and gloves. I had been wrong to think Grace's party would be fun. I had been wrong to think my mom would let me have a party today. The only thing I'd been right about was that people were mad at me. Things could not get any worse.

"Zeke, you look so sad. Let me cheer you up with a birthday kiss," Nicole Finkle said.

Then she kissed my cheek.

Yuck. I had been wrong about things not getting any worse. They just did.

Then Buffy Maynard tried to kiss my other cheek.

I turned away.

Her kiss missed my cheek. It landed on my lips.

Super yuck. I was sure things could not get any worse.

Then a bee flew near me.

Yikes! I had to stop thinking that things couldn't get any worse. Every time I thought that, things got worse.

I pounded on my front door and said, "Mom, please let me in. I have a good idea."

Mom said, "I told you I can't hold a party today. There are too many chores to do. I need to finish raking the backyard. And I have to sweep the floors and vacuum the rugs."

I told my mother my good idea: "We'll help you with the chores."

She opened the door.

Mia clapped her hands. "Yay! A party with big kids!"

Alexa crossed her arms. "Ugh. A party with little kids."

"Can you help us bake cupcakes?" I asked Alexa.

"Absolutely not," she said.

I held out the new nail polish I'd bought for Grace. "If you help us, I'll give you this nice bottle of nail polish."

Alexa looked at it. She said, "Ooh, that's pretty. Okay, I'll help you bake cupcakes."

Everyone made cupcakes together. We took turns adding the ingredients, stirring the batter, and spooning it into cupcake pans. I was the birthday boy, so I got to lick the bowl of batter. And it was awesome.

While the cupcakes baked, I made up a party game. I split everyone into two teams.

Team Awesome had to rake and bag the backyard leaves as fast as they could. Team Amazing had to vacuum the rugs as fast as they could.

It was a close game, with lots of excitement and great teamwork. In the end, Team Awesome won. I said, "Since Team Amazing lost, they have to sweep the floors."

"No fair," Nicole said.

"Why are you complaining? You're on Team Awesome. You won. You don't have to sweep our floors," I said.

"I'm complaining because I want to sweep the floors."

"Me too," Buffy said. "Raking with my friends was so much fun. I bet sweeping together will be fun too."

I faked a frown. Then I faked a sigh. Finally, I said, "Okay. Anyone who wants to can clean the floors."

Everyone cheered. Then they all swept the floors, taking turns with the brooms and dustpans.

Once the cupcakes came out of the oven, each person got one to frost, decorate, and eat.

I frosted mine with marshmallow sauce and decorated it with chocolate chips.

Hector frosted his cupcake with peanut butter. He topped it with stripes of jelly.

Victoria swirled applesauce on hers to make it look like a brain.

Rudy frosted his cupcake with ketchup. He topped it with bits of onion and garlic. "I love gross things," he said, talking with his mouth full.

In his mouth was a mixture of cupcake, ketchup, garlic, onion, and Rudy's spit. It was not a pretty sight.

We were still eating when the doorbell rang.

I walked to the front door and asked, "Who is it?"

"It's Grace Chang and my very long and very sharp and very evil fingernails."

"Yeah, it's Grace Chang. And Emma G.," Emma G. said.

"Yeah, it's Grace Chang. And Emma G. And Emma J.," Emma J. said.

"I'm in a very bad mood. I very much want to rip your face off," Grace said.

"In that case, you very much can't come in," I said.

"But you told me to let people in if they're not strangers. Grace Chang isn't a stranger," Mia said behind me.

I turned around. "Don't open that —"

Just as I was about to say "door," Mia opened the door.

Grace waved her very long, very sharp, and very evil fingernails in my face.

The Presence and Presents of Grace

"Please don't rip my face off. It's my birthday," I told Grace at my front door.

"You promised not to rip Zeke's face off until after his birthday," Hector pointed out.

"Good point," I said. "And if you rip my face off now, I won't give you a cupcake."

"Cupcake!" Grace licked her lips, hurried into the kitchen, and grabbed a cupcake.

Emma G. and Emma J. followed her. They each grabbed a cupcake too.

Grace spooned powdered sugar on her cupcake. Then she placed raisins on top of the sugar. She made raisin eyes, a raisin nose, and a frowning raisin mouth.

The Emmas made frowning raisin faces on their cupcakes too.

After Grace ate her cupcake, she walked out of the kitchen. She said, "You don't have entertainers like I had at my party. There's nothing to do here."

"Yeah. There's nothing to do here," Emma G. said.

"Yeah. There's nothing to do here," Emma J. said.

Nicole said, "We can entertain ourselves. Look what we just did."

She pointed to my dog, Waggles. He wore two skirts around his big, furry stomach.

Grace pointed to him. "Hey, those are the skirts I got for my birthday."

"You didn't want them, so we put them on Waggles," Buffy said. "And Zeke's big sister took the nail polish you didn't want. She let me polish Waggles's nails."

Waggles now had bright pink nails. On his head he wore a bow from one of Grace's presents. He looked ridiculous.

"Waggles is a boy dog," I protested.

The girls ignored me. Buffy petted Waggles and said, "What a pretty little sweetums."

Nicole petted Waggles and said, "You're the cutest smoochie woochie poochie."

Yuck. That made me want to vomit, emit emesis, puke, barf, ralph, yack, gack, hurl, launch lunch, blow chunks, yodel groceries, and — Rudy's personal favorite — laugh at the toilet.

Grace crossed her arms and said, "No fair. You did all the fun things without me. I didn't get to bake cupcakes or dress up the dog."

"We also got to rake leaves, vacuum the rugs, and sweep the floor," Laurie said.

"No fair." Grace stamped her foot.

"Yeah, no fair." Emma G. stamped her foot.

"Yeah, no fair." Emma J. stamped her foot.

Emma G. said, "Ow, that hurts."

Emma J. said, "Yeah, ow, that hurts."

"I'll let you girls play a fun new game called Clean the Kitchen," I said.

They cheered.

I rolled my eyes.

Grace and the Emmas put away all the cupcake ingredients, washed the dishes, and cleaned the kitchen counters. They thought they were playing a great party game.

I thought they were fools.

After that, everyone at the party did the jigsaw puzzle that Grace hadn't wanted.

I told Grace, "It's good to try new activities. You may think something will be bad. But once you do it, it's fun."

"Yes. Zeke thought a dance party would be bad. But dancing can be fun. Try it," Alexa said.

She taught everyone a dance called the Lost Chicken. We clucked, flapped our arms, and spun in circles.

Next, Mom taught us a dance called the Bump. We bumped our butts together.

Then we made up our own dances. Mine was called Angry Dude. I crossed my arms, stomped my foot, and shook my head, all at the same time.

I had to admit that dancing was a lot more fun than I'd thought it would be.

"Zeke also thought a Princess Sing-Along party would be bad. But Princess Sing-Along can be fun," my sister Mia said. "Listen to this great song: Keep your room clean like you've been told, la la la. Unless you want to sleep with mold, la la la. You may enjoy eating lunch meat, la la la, but won't like it under your sheet, la la la."

"I tried listening to Princess Sing-Along. It wasn't fun," I said.

Everyone but Rudy agreed with me. He said, "Princess Sing-Along's song about sleeping with lunch meat is really gross. So it's great."

"We may not agree on everything, but I think we all agree that Zeke's party has been fantastic," Hector said.

Everyone agreed.

Turning nine was a lot better than I'd expected.

Then Owen Leach said, "Zeke's party has been fantastic. But my party tomorrow at Thrillsville will be even better."

"Yay! I can't wait to ride the Thrill-o-coaster," Buffy said.

"And the Splash Attack," Nicole added.

"I want to see the new Fabo-Awesome show," Charlie said.

Rudy rubbed his belly. "I want to eat a bucket of Thrillsville's Famous Fried Fat. Then I'll go on a fast ride and try to barf on it. It'll be so cool."

For a few minutes, everyone seemed to forget about my party, even while they were at my party.

At least I wouldn't forget about my party. I thought it was the best party ever.

Laundry Folding: Almost as Good as Thrillsville

IS THIS HEART ON A ROLLER COASTER?!

When I woke up the next day, my heart boomed with excitement. Soon I'd be at Owen's party at Thrillsville.

Then I heard another booming noise: thunder. Uh-oh.

I also heard the sound of pouring rain.

Then I heard the ringing of our phone and the chiming of our doorbell.

I walked out of my bedroom to find out who was calling and who was at the door.

Mom answered the phone in the living room. She was wearing her old bathrobe. Her hair stuck out all over the place. Dark circles lumped under her eyes. She must have just woken up.

I heard her say, "What? Again? You've got to be kidding me," into the phone.

The doorbell kept ringing.

I went to the door and said, "Who's there?"

"Owen," Owen said.

"Shouldn't you be at home, waiting for your party to start?" I asked.

"That's what my mom is talking to your mom about on the phone," he said.

I opened the door. Owen was there. Behind him were a bunch of kids from our class. They all shouted:

"That's nice of you to have a surprise party for me. But I just had a party yesterday," I said.

"Actually, we're surprising you with a party for me. Can I have my birthday party here?" Owen asked. "We had so much fun at your house yesterday. And we can't go to Thrillsville today. It's closed because of the thunder and lightning."

I said, "Lightning? What light —"

A big bolt of lightning flashed in the sky.

"So can I have my party at your house today?" Owen asked. "We can do more dance moves with your sister."

I shrugged.

"And we'll let Mia sing another Princess Sing-Along song," Nicole said.

I shrugged again.

"And we can dress up your dog in adorable
outfits," Buffy said.

"No," I said.

"Okay, we'll leave the dog alone," Buffy
said.

Mom came to the door.

"Thanks a lot," she said. She didn't seem very thankful. "I'm glad you had fun here yesterday. But I have a lot to do today. I have laundry to fold and floors to mop," she said.

"Perfect. We'll have a laundry-folding and floor-mopping contest," I said. "Mom, now that I'm older, I'll take over some of the chores from now on. Doing chores with friends can be fun."

Mom smiled. "Zeke, you have really matured. You're older and wiser. You deserve a bigger allowance and a later bedtime."

I thanked her. Turning nine had worked out great after all.

Then I let everyone into the house. After I got my friends to fold the laundry and mop the floor, maybe I could have them clean my room too.

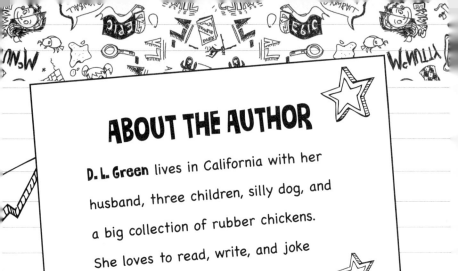

ABOUT THE AUTHOR

D. L. Green lives in California with her husband, three children, silly dog, and a big collection of rubber chickens. She loves to read, write, and joke around.

ABOUT THE ILLUSTRATOR

Josh Alves gets to celebrate his birthday on Thanksgiving (occasionally) and loves ice cream cake (regularly). Josh gets to draw in his studio in Maine where he lives with his amazing wife and three incredible children.

CAN A BIRTHDAY PARTY AT HOME BE FUN?

(And other really important questions)

Write answers to these questions, or discuss them with your friends and classmates.

1. Can a birthday party at home be fun? If so, what sort of things make it fun?

2. Does having a big, fancy party guarantee it will be incredible? How do you know?

3. What sort of birthday gifts do you like to give your friends? Do you like to go shopping for them, or do you just want your mom to pick something up for you?

4. Imagine you could go anywhere for your party and do anything you want. Where would you go, and what would you do?

BIG WORDS
according to Zeke

TRY USING THEM IN SENTENCES JUST LIKE I DO

ADORABLE: A word that girls use to describe things that they think are super cute. But adorable things are actually usually annoying and somewhat gross.

ALLOWANCE: The money you get from your parents, usually for helping out around the house. People like Grace Chang probably don't have to do anything for their allowance.

EMBARRASSING: Something that makes people laugh at you until you feel weird and want to go hide.

EMESIS: The doctor-approved word for throwing up.

EMIT: To give off or throw out, like a stink or puke.

ENCYCLOPEDIA: A book or web site that has information about EVERYTHING and EVERYBODY. Victoria Crow is a walking encyclopedia.

ENTERTAINERS: People who do interesting things that make you ooo and ahh and clap really hard.

FANTASTIC: Really great and amazing, like the Bloody Gore video game, roller coasters, and cupcakes.

GIGANTIC: Super-duper huge.

INVITATIONS: The cards you send when you are going to have a party. They tell all the information about your party, like date, time, and place.

IT DOESN'T GET ANY MORE RIDICULOUS THAN WAGGLES WEARING A BONNET!

MAGICIAN: A person who does tricks that amaze kids, unless they are the lamest magician ever, like the one at Grace's party. Then they just make kids boo.

MATURE: Grown up and ready to stay up later and get a bigger allowance.

MUSEUM: A place that is filled with collections and displays that are usually pretty cool. You tend to learn a lot at museums, but they are still fun.

MUTANT: An animal or person that has changed somehow so that it becomes a sort of monster. Mutants are completely awesome.

RIDICULOUS: Very silly and just not right, like Waggles in girly clothes.

SHUDDERED: Shook out of fear, like when Grace Chang waves her fingernails at me.

TREMBLING: Shaking, usually out of fear, like when a bug comes anywhere within five feet of you.

UNIVERSE: All of the planets and stars and outer space everything all together. In other words, a really huge area.

Party Like You're in Argentina!

This game is a classic party game from Argentina! It takes a little more planning than I had time for before my surprise-Mom birthday party. But it is totally worth the effort. Everyone will be rolling on the floor laughing by the end, and you can wow your friends by telling them you know how Argentinians like to party.

What you need:

- small party gifts — enough so everyone can have one

- a box that is big enough to hold the party gifts

- 10 slips of paper

- a pen

- wrapping paper

- a stereo or something that plays music

What you do:

1. Before the party, write a dare on each slip of paper. Be crazy and creative. "Lick your own foot," and, "Sing 'I'm a Little Teapot,' " are good examples.

2. Place the party gifts in the box and wrap it.

3. Attach a dare note to the outside of the box, then wrap it again. Repeat this step until all the notes are hidden within the layers of wrapping paper.

4. At the party, have everyone stand in a circle. Ask an adult to run the music. As the music plays, pass the package around the circle.

5. When the music stops, stop passing the package. The person holding the box must unwrap one layer and do the dare. (See why you want the dares to be crazy?)

6. Keep going until the box is all unwrapped and the party gifts are revealed. Everyone shares the gifts!

The party doesn't have to stop here!

THE COOLEST GUY YOU'LL EVER MEET

Zeke Meeks

My hair looks awesome!

HELP

OWEN, THE POPULAR PHONY

VERY CONFUSED BEST FRIEND

...AKA STINKY

VS THE PUTRID PUPPET PALS

BY D.L. GREEN

More like ENEMIES!

MOST BORING TOY EVER MADE

THE COOLEST GUY YOU'LL EVER MEET

Zeke Meeks

This hat cramps my style

HE GIVES MAGICIANS A BAD NAME

SO LAME HIS RABBIT IS BORED

He's trying hard NOT to ROLL my dice

VS THE BIG BLAH-RIFIC BIRTHDAY

BY D. L. GREEN

AKA FULL OF AWFUL, AWKWARD MOMENTS

Like any time spent with Grace Chang

THRILLSVILLE!

JOIN

Zeke Meeks

in all his hilarious adventures!

Seriously.

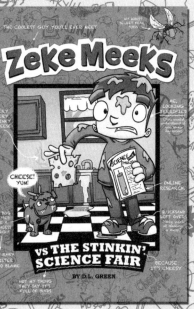

Have the next book ready...

SET... GO!!

AWESOME HAIR

CHARMING SMILE

Zeke Meeks

COOLEST THIRD GRADER YOU'LL EVER MEET!